The Early Years

David Kernot

Published by David Kernot, 2013.

THE EARLY YEARS

First edition. April 28, 2013.

Copyright © 2013 David Kernot.

ISBN: 979-8231145102

Written by David Kernot.

Table of Contents

To my wife, Olivia, who lets me dream, always!

DEAD MAN WALKING

Jonah walked to his car and put the bomb threat that he and the team had received aside. Right now it all seemed far removed. Acknowledging it gave it power and left unchecked would disable him. He refused to give it credibility. If he did the terrorists had already won. He stopped as the deep rumble of a shuttle launch intensified, drowned the chorus of birds. He shivered and pulled his jacket tighter. Had he imagined the ground shake? He didn't think so.

Towards the spaceport, a shuttle appeared, it rose above the local houses and climbed higher, positioned itself for the next stage. Jonah watched the white glow, and held his breath, waited, dared not blink.

What would it be like to be crew right now? Tucked inside the craft as it shook and fought to break free from Earth's shackles? No doubt, it would be exciting to be given the opportunity.

Still, held in suspension, while the Faster-Than-Light engines propelled the ship across the universe, was worthwhile.

One day, he would be part of the crew and travel the universe in search of new life.

He stood, shielded his eyes, and a tickle of excitement ran through him. The sky turned brilliant white as the ship's FTL drive engaged. He closed his eyes, and the inverse black and white image faded. A second later he heard the sonic boom. "God speed," he whispered. He scanned the empty sky. "One day, I'll be up there too."

With the renewed chorus of the birds sheltered from morning frost, reality returned. There'd be no interstellar travel, no adventures in space.

He pushed away the thoughts. He had family now, other responsibilities. There was no room for the wild and irresponsible dreams of his youth. How could he contemplate leaving them? He loved them both more than life itself. They were his life.

Jonah sighed and climbed into the car. The BMW Frontier had been modeled on the next version of spacecraft to head into space—the Delphini Probes—sleek, fitted with state of the art technology.

He turned off the radio report on partial DNA cloning and smiled as he remembered his pleasure over breakfast. They had reviewed his research on the selective gene modeling of artificial flesh over the endoskeleton of androids. He had expected the news flash—until then a closely guarded secret—but there were elements not released, such as his name. He leaned over and opened the car's glove box, pulled out two small, sterilized containers. He examined his suit jacket, pulled a single strand of long blonde hair from it, and placed it into one container. Meticulous, he collected each hair for the next phase of his research, even though he already had enough DNA for the gene sequencer. He did the same—this time searching for short hair, tinged with red—and placed them into the other container. He allowed himself a smug smile. Even if he didn't travel into space, Linda and Martin's DNA—and his—would seed new worlds with human DNA. He put on his seatbelt and drove to work.

JONAH SMILED ACROSS the kitchen at Linda. "Let's go on a holiday."

Linda paused in mid-stride, her eyes narrowed. "Now?"

Jonah noticed her long, striking eyelashes and couldn't help but grin. "Yes! Let's drop everything and go away for a few weeks."

She clicked her fingers. "Just like that? I asked you a month ago, and you said you couldn't consider a holiday."

"I did?"

"Yes!"

"I honestly don't remember... Let's do it anyway!" he added excitedly.

"No!" She folded her arms. "I can't just pull Martin out of school. What are you thinking?"

Excitement dissipated. "I thought it would be nice to go on a holiday, just the three of us. I'll school him while we're away."

"Oh, no! You're the scientist. What is it you're always telling me? That you can never get away, you're too important." She raised her hands. "What's suddenly changed?"

Jonah shrank under her gaze. He shrugged and wondered what to say. How could he say that it was just because he loved her and wanted to spend time with them both?

"Aren't you working on some big project?"

He cleared his throat. "I've got a seminar to go to. Why don't you come with me and we can relax after that?"

"Really?"

"You know we're close to finishing up the human genome sequencing. The team over at 454 Life Sciences are so confident with us they want some payload on the fifth Delphini Probe, the first one to take humans all the way out into space."

Linda looked surprised and sat on the sofa. "I had no idea. They must be pleased."

"They are," he said, puffing out his chest. "The Delphini Probes will grow a new world, out in M5142, from a seed bank of human DNA." He held up his hands. "It's experimental stuff. We don't know how it will go."

"You should take my DNA, and put it in that seed bank," she teased.

"I already have." He grinned, remembering his daily ritual of collecting hair samples.

"You stole my DNA?"

"I didn't steal it, I took those long, blonde, hairs you're always leaving on my suit." He laughed over her shocked expression. "Then stop kissing me before work. Anyway, it's too late to get it back. You've already been processed in the gene sequencer!"

"I suppose you've put yourself in there too."

He laughed. "Can't have you meeting somebody else, now could I? Just imagine it... We could meet up again as cloned life forms on a different world and fall in love all over again."

She laughed, picked up a cushion, and threw it at him. It bounced harmlessly off his head. "Jonah, you're such a romantic idiot."

He rubbed his head, joking as if in pain from the cushion. "So, what about this holiday?"

"What about the team?"

"They won't have it finished for a few months yet, they can do without me for a few weeks."

She paused. "No, there's something else. I've noticed a change. You're not giving up on space travel?"

He didn't know what to say.

"What about your dream? To clamber aboard one of those spaceships. Explore unknown worlds?"

Jonah sighed. How could he tell her he was running away, that he had learned that the bomb threat to the team had been confirmed as credible? There were people out there that didn't want to give power to the development of androids. Taking time off would get him away.

"I don't know," he said. "I guess I'm too old for that now."

Linda walked over to him.

He breathed in her perfume while she cradled his face in her hands.

"Jonah, my darling, never give up on your dreams. It makes you who you are. You have so much ambition and you've worked hard on this project. You can't give up now."

There was a long comfortable silence between them. Then she walked to the door and called up the stairs. "Martin, Daddy said we're going on a holiday."

A sound accompanied "Hooray!" Martin's reply from the other room, and not unlike a herd of stampeding elephants.

Jonah smiled at the excitable five-year-old when he entered the room.

THE LIGHT SPLINTERED on the fresh cedar leaves that lined the quiet suburban street, and the colorful shards of light sparkled across the BMW Frontier. Jonah packed the last suitcase and clambered into the driver's seat. As Linda climbed into the car he raised his eyebrows, and a tremor of excitement ran through him. "Ready?" Jonah knew it didn't matter that he had thought of everything imaginable, there would be something he'd forgotten: a toothbrush for Martin, Linda's favorite pair of shoes. He waited for her to run through the list.

"I'm ready." She grinned. "Let's go."

He threw Linda a smile, and he reversed the car down the drive and off onto the road.

"Jonah, I've got something to tell you."

"Ah ha." He nodded, didn't take his eyes from the slippery road.

"I'm pregnant."

"What?" A jolt of excitement ran through him and he gripped the steering wheel tighter. He glanced sideways. "How?"

Linda sniggered. "The usual way, silly."

"Sorry... Yes, but how? How long have you known?"

"A little while now. I was going to say something earlier, but you've been so absent minded with your project. I thought you would have noticed the change in me." She rubbed her stomach. "I had a scan yesterday afternoon."

"Yesterday! I wondered what all the secrecy was about." It all made sense now, the mood swings, the odd comments here and there. "How did it go?"

"Good. Everything's fine. It's a girl. We will have a little sister for Martin."

"Wow!" He wanted to lower the side window and yell out the news at the top of his voice but he focused on the heavy rain, took his foot off the accelerator. He set the car to automatic—it could handle the wet conditions better than he—then faced Linda. "When is she due? Have we got enough clothes? Is our house big enough?"

Linda pulled a face. "So many questions!"

"Wow! I will be a father again," he said proudly. "Wait until I tell the guys at work."

"No doubt they'll want more DNA for your space project?" Linda raised her eyebrows.

"No." He shivered from the cold and turned up the heater again, glanced to a thick wall of cloud up ahead. "Actually, just imagine if we got created on another extra-terrestrial world, and we, I mean they, have children. They should all have similar DNA to our children here on Earth."

"Well, you'd better keep up your stellar navigation study if you want to be crew on that big fancy ship of yours. Keep scribbling down those weird formulas. It's the only way that you can visit your other children." She smiled. "After you're done with your seminar, the holiday will really begin."

JONAH WALKED OUT ONTO the podium and presented his speech at the seminar. He looked at the time, and cleared his throat. Twenty minutes and their holiday began.

He smiled to Linda and Martin, down in the front row, and leaned closer to the podium.

He began his summation of the development of the latest model android.

"Welcome, distinguished guests to the wonderful history of the Model 8205 Android—"

"Lies!" A man to the right of Linda stood up.

There was a bright flash.

The wall of shrapnel that followed threw Jonah off his feet.

In a heartbeat, Linda and Martin were gone, and the darkness took him.

UNCHARTED DEEP SPACE. On board the fifth Delphini Probe, The Aurora Glen:

Linda and Martin were why he had pushed ahead with his research and been able to store their DNA. It was why he had created an android in Linda's likeness. Linda would have given her blessing. One day she would. He would never give up. It was why he didn't sleep and why he could sense the distance from Earth increase as the Aurora Glen sped through the vacuum of space. She was the fifth Delphini Probe. The first to carry human passengers to the outer edges of the solar system and explore unfamiliar worlds out on the rim. All but essential crew were asleep in their crypt-like stasis tubes, safe for five years in space.

The Aurora Glen responded as chunks of space debris peppered its hull. Air leaked into the void of space. Damaged CO_2 scrubbers failed, left the air untreated. The automatic outer sections sealed as oxygen levels fell. Alarms activated.

Jonah's feed from the ship's computer provided the information clinically. Only for Jonah, caught in the pseudo, dream-like state of the stasis tubes, these fragments of information became intertwined with other images. The shrill alarms faded as a drug-induced sleep took hold.

The machine-generated white noise failed to hold him in a deep, dream-like state. Images pulled at him. The satisfied look from the anti-android movement suicide bomber who stepped onto the stage.

Screams in a crowded room. Linda's silenced cry as shrapnel tore her apart. Martin in a pool of his own blood. The images never left him. Jonah clenched and unclenched his prosthetic left hand, over and over, as the nightmares returned unabated.

Jonah blinked as painful bright light forced his eyes shut. The chaotic white noise ceased. Life support restraints released him. He reached down and clipped the two large titanium cylinders that contained Martin and Linda's DNA and their farmed memories onto each side of his belt.

Outside, there was no familiar sound of the crew. No jovial laughter. Only a shrill alarm. The travel drugs were still in his system, so it couldn't be arrival time. He twisted to face the readout on the wall and blinked life back into his eyes. "Christ!" The curse ignited a volley of coughs. "Reading steady on three point two light years." The words sounded forced, as if someone had replaced his tongue with a flat, dry stone. "We're nowhere near M5142." He calculated three absent light years, and disbelief flowed through him. "I've woken thirty months early!" He activated the switch on his belt, started a voice recorder. "Jonah Masters." He cringed and swallowed hard. "Imperial identity... one seven eight... five one three... dash two. Alarm heard on stasis deck. Current time..." He paused. It didn't matter, and he switched off the recorder. He forced his way out of the stasis tube. There was no time for protocol.

On the Stasis Deck the alarm deafened. He crossed the sparse ill-lit floor, hands over his ears, and stumbled into a table and fell. The titanium DNA tubes clattered, loud against the tiled floor, and Jonah threw up. He heaved until there was nothing left of the cocktail of drugs and hibernation fluids. He wiped the trail of bile from his face and slammed on the recorder. "There's been a breach! High ozone present on the Stasis Deck!"

He glanced over to Raph's stasis tube, peppered with holes, and wondered what could have caused the damage.

They had mapped the trip with incredible precision; he had helped plot the trajectories. There had been no asteroid belts, comets, or suns in their flight path.

All the crew's stasis tubes were pocked with small holes. He had been lucky enough to be hidden away in a corner out of the way. Eleven outstanding men and women never stood a chance. His best friend, Raph, gone.

Jonah cut a path to the nearest intercom. "Bridge, Jonah here."

There was only silence.

"Damn it!" He dialed again. "Linda! Are you there?"

More silence.

"Linda!" He wondered what to do next.

"Jonah?" A faint voice crackled over the intercom.

"Thank heavens!"

"Jonah, I tried Raph, but he never answered. Nobody did."

"Raph's dead!"

There was no reply.

"They're all dead, Linda! The whole crew. Where are you?"

"Trapped by the Bridge. The crew are gone."

"What happened?"

"Radiation shower. Meteors or something. Put on a suit and come up. The ship's hull is damaged and air will vent if we take another direct hit!"

"Roger that." He pulled on a protective spacesuit from a nearby cabinet, and grabbed a first aid kit, before he headed up to the Bridge. He forced life into his lethargic body as he pressed his way up the four flights of stairs. Halfway up, part of the stairwell was missing. Molten charred metal lay strewn amongst the twisted wreckage. Jonah jumped over it, scrambled onto a solid section, and hurried to the Bridge level.

Linda was on her back, her leg missing below the knee. Blood oozed from the stump. "Jesus!" He ran over and cradled her head in his arms.

"Jonah," she cried, and tried to sit up. "The FTL drive is still active! I couldn't reach it. It needs to be shut down!"

Jonah scrambled through the wreckage to a panel on the wall, leaned into the retina scanner, and punched in a series of numbers on the keypad. The light changed to green as he slammed his palm on the drive button.

The sound of the ship's drives changed. They slowed. The shrill alarm quieted a fraction.

"It's done. Don't move." His hands shook while he struggled to open the First Aid Kit and apply a tourniquet. The bleeding around the stump slowed, and he injected her with a cocktail of quick acting painkillers. "What happened?"

"I got caught in the stairs, trying to avoid whatever penetrated the ship."

"You're amazing. I don't know how you stayed awake all this time. How did you get past that molten metal on the stairs? Get back here to contact Raph?"

She shrugged. "I needed to get to the Bridge."

He glanced to the Bridge. From there, they could get to the nearest Life Pod Station.

"Carry me to Bridge controls and then go. You have your precious titanium tubes to worry about."

Surprised, he looked at her. She had to be delirious. She had just lost her leg.

She nodded. "Look at you. Sorry I snapped, you look terrible."

"I look terrible?"

"Why so glum?"

"I plotted the trajectories myself. If anyone's to blame for this, it's me."

"It's nobody's fault, Jonah. Space travel is dangerous. Anything can happen. You can't plan for every eventuality."

"No," he agreed.

"Again, help me to the Bridge."

He nodded, carried her over to the door, and pressed the access code. The door hissed open, and they entered.

Through the gigantic window, the vista of space glistened. Far away stars twinkled. Gassy nebulous matter pulsed with energy from the nearby formation.

"Jonah! Look at the shape of it, and the range of colors!"

He stepped closer, speechless.

Like a jewel in the sky, the enormous doughnut-shaped disk, whirled. Filled with a kaleidoscope of colors, it ebbed and flowed in a complex, yet beautiful, hypnotic pattern. Radiation poured out from the middle, and every time just missed the ship. Random bolts of light shot from its core, spun off in all directions.

"Now we know what damaged the ship," she said.

"Whatever it is, it's pulling us into its center."

"I'll check the database."

"We should go." His hands fumbled at the titanium tubes by his side.

She ignored him and leaned forward and entered commands into a console.

Reluctant, he waited.

A nearby screen flickered into life, as another random burst of energy burst from the center of the space doughnut shape.

"Jonah, look at this, it's uncharted! We can catalogue it as G124-A1. It will be ours forever."

Another bolt of energy shot past, and he cringed. "We haven't got time to send a message."

"Look at it." She ignored him and read from the screen. "A sun twenty-five times bigger than Earth's. Scan it with the Doppler Shift Radar, will you?"

"We need to get into a Life Pod!"

"Jonah, I can't walk by myself. Just press the Doppler switch for me!"

"Can't you hear the alarm? The ship will get hit by an energy bolt or run out of air at any moment. Forget the radar!"

"I don't care. I've had plenty of time up here, light years, to think. Our mission was to seed new worlds! Start up the radar, and then you can find your Life Pod. I want to see what's in that disk."

He stalked over to the Doppler Panel and pressed several buttons. As he strode back, the screen lit up beside her.

"We are drifting into its core, but you'll never guess." She smiled.

"What?" He felt impatient, and gripped the titanium tubes, eager to get to a Pod.

"There are four new 'C' class planets out there!"

"What size?" His interest grew as he put aside the alarms and her unusual hostility.

"Three Jovian size and a smaller one, all high in methane, nitrogen, but no measurable oxygen, and tagged as potentially suitable for life."

"How's that possible? None of this was here when we left Earth."

She shrugged. "It's here now. Taking into account the lesser gravity of the sun and approximating equivalent distances, the smallest is one point two Earth Units, out in an elliptical orbit." Her face took on a prophetic look. "It's perfect for us, Jonah! We should seed it!"

He laughed, but it sounded hollow, and he shook his head. "At another time... If the ship wasn't so damaged." He marched over to her and held her hands. "Don't, there's no time?"

"I'm staying. It's why we came. To create new life, to seed other planets."

He reached for the titanium tubes by his side. To Linda and Martin, their lives held in limbo. He couldn't sacrifice himself; give up on a chance to bring them back. He needed to get to a Life Pod.

Unsure what to say, how to convince her, he hesitated and watched her mouth set in a line that suggested she had decided.

The ship's life support system whooped loudly. An imminent sign. "Quickly, Linda, we have to go."

"I'm staying. I will seed this system. Think of the lives I can create."

The alarm deafened. "There isn't time to discuss this. Come with me."

"No! You go."

"Why?"

"I'll never forget you, I'm grateful for what you did, but it's not enough. So go!"

"Sure. Forever grateful. Whatever. You'll be dead in under ten minutes if you don't come now."

"Go to a Life Pod. I'll stay and build you a planet full of people to land on."

"No!" He stepped forward, confused.

Her eyes glistened. Part of him could see there was value in seeding a new colony of life. It was the culmination of his work on the project. Martin's and Linda's DNA was in the seed bank. "Come with me," he urged.

"No! You're damaged goods, Jonah. You've never appreciated me. Your focus has always been on those tubes. For your other Linda, and Martin. Anyway, I'm not Linda, I'm L-I-N-D-A." She emphasized every syllable. "I'm a robot, bio-engineered for god's sake."

"No, you're real," he insisted.

"I'm only part flesh. Go on Jonah, stop fooling yourself. You've got your Linda and Martin in those tubes. Take them, and fight for all your lives. Bring them back to life. You've never given yourself to me. Never!"

Jonah's temper ignited. "They were my family. I took them somewhere and got them killed. I was responsible! What did you expect me to do? Forget them? Say they never existed." His eyes burned as he clenched his hands.

Her voice was quiet, each sentence metered out precisely. "Get to a Life Pod. I'll seed for as long as I can. My robotic body can withstand more than your pathetic human one."

Tears welled, and his stomach knotted. "I won't leave you!"

"Jonah, grow up! I'm not her! I'm not, Linda. I never was! You might have made me look like her; I might be from her DNA. Yes, I have her implanted memories, but I would never be your dead wife."

She paused, and he could see that she tried to take some sting out of her words. "What does L-I-N-D-A stand for?"

"Advanced Generation Systems Linux Interactive Navigational Device Assembly." He swallowed hard and wiped away the tears. She was bio-engineered from titanium steel, the smallest Linux kernel his money could buy, covered in real cultured flesh.

Her eyes blazed. "Correct. I'm not human. I'm just a machine. Now go!" She put her hands on his shoulders and pushed him away, before she turned and entered a series of commands into the terminal.

Jonah realized she was right. He had never given her a chance. He had focused on Linda and Martin. It was why he was on board the Aurora Glen. He nodded and ran to the far door, towards the closest Life Pod. He pressed the button got an alarm. It was jammed. He pushed again, but it didn't move.

The other Pods were on the opposite side of the ship. He would have to hurry. He ran past Linda without a glance. They had said enough.

He ran along damaged corridors, scrambled towards freedom, the whooping of the ship's alarm more insistent with every step.

Another bolt of gamma radiation shook the ship. It felt close to the Bridge, but he knew there was nothing he could do. They would release seed from the cargo into the ring of the developing nebulae. All the elements of mankind were there; one hundred thousand different stands of RNA and DNA, complete with an accelerant. The oxygen-producing bacteria would feed on methane gas and help sow mankind's seed all over again. It was a man-made Panspermia!

But halfway to the Pods, he slowed. An image swam into his mind, of the day he, Martin, and Linda had left on a holiday together. Linda was wearing one of her contagious smiles as she stepped into the car, and colorful shards of light bounced from her hair.

He grinned at her, and he realized no matter what he did, she would never come back. The person he would create from the titanium tubes would not be her, any more than the Linda he left at the Bridge.

He was wrong. Why hadn't he realized that before? He was no less a man just because they had fitted him with an android's prosthetic arm. Linda did not differ from him in that regard.

He turned and ran back towards the Bridge. To Linda. He understood he had just committed suicide. There would be no more opportunities to get to a Life Pod. There would be no chance to bring Linda and Martin back.

Jonah burst onto the Bridge. Linda sat on a chair. She worked on the seeding console. "I'm an idiot," he yelled. "Life isn't anything without you. I love you." He ran over and caressed her. "I've just been too much of a fool to realize it. I don't care that you're not like Linda."

A tear ran down her face, and she smiled.

At that point the ship's alarm became unbearable as it announced the end of the air supply.

"Quickly." He glanced at the far door. "There's no time to get to the other Life Pods, we have to get this door open. I must break away the control panel."

He ran over and kicked at the panel. It didn't budge. He tried prizing it open with his fingers. It wouldn't open.

Filled with frustration, he yelled, "Ahhhhhhh! I don't have a screwdriver."

He clawed at the panel again. Blood ran from his torn fingers, as he tried to pry the cover away, until light headed from the lack of air, he fell to the floor. The titanium tubes clattered, loud on the floor.

An idea formed, and he closed his eyes in despair.

Anything but that.

But there was no alternative.

Kill or die.

He forced himself up, unclipped one of the titanium tubes, and smashed the door controls. The tube split in two before the panel gave way, and Linda's contents spilled over the door. He unclipped Martin's tube, tried not to think of him, and set at the door again. Tears fell freely. Martin's tube ruptured, but it didn't matter anymore. He continued smashing at the panel and understood Linda and Martin could never come back.

He had held on to their memories too tight.

It had affected his life with Linda.

That hadn't been fair. Even androids had feelings.

A part of him said he shouldn't let go.

Not to forget.

And he continued his onslaught.

The panel buckled.

He ripped away the panel, disabled the locks and opened the door.

He ran back and picked up Linda.

"They are both out there," she whispered. "Their DNA seeded these other planets. You've got your wish, Jonah. They will live again," she said, and wiped away his tears.

She wiped away his tears while he held her.

He nodded, filled with mixed emotions, but took comfort in the way she snuggled into him.

"I love you." She whispered in his ear, "We can have children of our own, you know. I'm more than capable."

An excited tremor ran through him as he carried her through the open doorway, toward the safety of the Life Pods. His mind exploded with the fresh opportunities their lives together offered. He just had to reach the Pods in time, transmit a message, and then wait for the next Delphini Probe to arrive. It seemed so simple.

He never looked back to where the titanium tubes remained, abandoned on the floor.

THE SCARLET RUNNERS

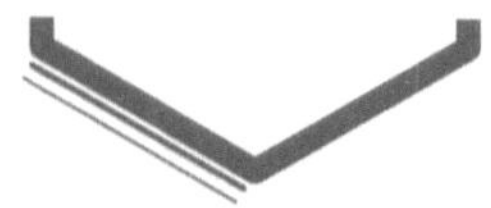

Doris shuffled across their kitchen, scuffed up the worn linoleum, and slopped her habitual brown dishwater into James' mug as he scanned the evening news pages. She was the perfect wife, loving and forgetful, but he couldn't fathom why the scalding fluid always smelled like coffee and varied in taste from cabbage to ashtrays. He barely noticed today's flavour—crab sticks—as his eyes lit at the page three announcements: and an advertisement for a plot in Hades. 'Space Filling Fast', it suggested.

James chuckled. "Look at this, dear."

Doris ambled over and he uncurled an arthritic finger and pointed to the advert.

"That's nice, dear." Doris' tone didn't change its squeaky pitch, and she ambled back to the sink of soaking dishes.

What was it with those conspiracy theorists? It's always something different each week. A not-so-subtle Mayan reminder to the end of the world. He couldn't wait for 2012 to be over. But if they were right, then two days was all anyone had. It was rubbish.

He pushed back his chair and stood up, made a mental note to go down to the corner store and buy Doris something nice for Christmas. A thick pair of socks, or a cardigan would do, and a box of Mayland's dark chocolates so she could sit by the fire and suck on the gooey centres without her teeth in.

"Doris, I'm going out for some fresh air, I'll look over my runner beans, see if we have enough for a meal."

"A meal of Scarlet Runners would be nice, considering the time you spend out in that garden of yours, dear."

"They were Dad's pride and joy, Doris, you know that. You've seen the price of vegetables, I'm saving us money by growing our own."

"So you've said. Don't get too cold, dear. Say hello to the moon for me."

She didn't turn as he left the room.

OUTSIDE, JAMES SET up his telescope—a ten-inch Meade with an Equatorial mount—and focused through the clouds at the Pleiades constellation. If the end of the world was coming in two days, then something should happen out that way.

He counted each of the sisters and shuddered.

"Eight?"

There was an extra one.

"How?"

One star brightened, grew larger through the viewfinder. It filled his field of view. It had to be an asteroid, a comet, or a meteorite. Even a piece of space junk would explain the speed at which it moved. He stepped back from the telescope and looked up, blinked rapidly to readjust his eyes to the night sky. Transfixed, he chewed his lip, watched the object grow in a mesmerizing fashion, bigger and closer with every breath, until it filled his field of view again. But this time he wasn't looking through a telescope.

At the last moment he jumped aside. "Curse it!" He felt the heat singe his face as it ploughed into his favourite patch of scarlet runner beans, pulverised them with barely a thud.

An illusion. Not that big after all. Or had it shrunk through space? Slightly larger than his hand, it sat nestled in his vegetable patch amongst pulverised beans. Steam hissed from it.

No! They were his dad's bean seed, his father's pride and joy and thanks to a shortage of bees last season, there were only a handful of seed left. He reacted before rational thought kicked in, and he reached in and tapped the rock away from the remaining runners, along past his courgettes, around the rhubarb and then out of the vegetable patch onto the lawn where it continued to hiss.

He felt giddy, his mind clouded with a compulsion and he bent down and picked it up, mindless to the pain as it burned slowly through his flesh. He knew what was happening. He struggled to let go, but he couldn't.

Then wave upon wave of emotion assaulted him.

Acidity tore at his nostrils.

And an unbearable cacophony filled him, as if he had tuned into every radio station around the globe.

Ghostly images appeared; of a tall race that lived peacefully in a twisted wood. They were shaded by leaves that constantly shimmered, changed shape and size, and pulsated with colours, purple, yellow and red.

In his mind, James saw a pale man.

He turned to James. "Stay away from Calycium! We are worlds apart!"

James fell backwards, landed between two cauliflowers, and let go of the meteorite.

It rolled between his legs, too close for comfort, and he scrabbled backwards.

The man's image faded, and with it the coloured, beautiful landscape.

The compulsion not to scream out in pain faded. But as he stared down at his crimson forearm, he felt nothing in his blackened hand.

He stood and walked over to his garden shed, rummaged through the drawers until he found a thick gardening glove, and a large, square-metal biscuit box. It was almost as old as him.

He upended the box and let the contents fall out: a clump of old twine, a collection of old black and whites—of Doris by the seaside—and seeds he had meant to plant out a few years back.

He put on the glove and walked outside.

This time when he picked up the meteorite there was no emotional outpouring, no strange images.

He stowed it in the metal box and placed it at the back of his shed, under a pile of gardening magazines, and then trudged inside.

Upstairs, he stopped at his bedroom door.

Doris sat up and turned on her lamp. "What is that god awful smell, James?"

He forced a smile.

She'd put rollers in her hair and white face-cream on, but she was still beautiful.

"I've been burning incense to celebrate the end of the world, dear. It's Myrrh." It was all a lie. He could hardly tell her it was burnt flesh. "I found a meteorite, dear. It came all the way from the Pleiades to see us. Only just missed me."

She screwed up her face and looked like a prune. "That's nice. But the incense reeks, James. Take it back outside."

"Yes, dear," he replied thankful she didn't have her glasses on, and he continued to the far bedroom, all the while he looked at his red arm.

How was it he could have heard voices, seen strange images? What was it about that meteorite?

He dressed his arm in salve and bandages, and by the time he returned to their bedroom Doris was asleep.

It wouldn't be right to wake her again, and she might comment on the smell of his arm again, so he decided not to kiss her goodnight—the first time in living memory since their marriage—and turned away from her disappointed.

JAMES WOKE EARLY.

At breakfast he absently moved food around the plate with a spoon, unable to ignore the withered fingers under the bandage. He rang Martin and collected the biscuit tin from the shed before leaving. It was still early, and Doris slept.

Martin met him at the door. "What's that god awful smell, James?"

He held up his blackened arm. "I burnt it."

"You should have that seen to, James. You can die from a burn that size. Does it hurt?"

James shook his head. "Sadly not."

"Give me a moment. You need a doctor."

Martin returned a little while later. "It's settled then. I've made an appointment with my doctor—on the High Street—he's very good. You should go while I—" He looked at the metal box and frowned. "What is it you want me to do?"

"I need you to look at something, a rock that fell into my garden."

"A fallen rock?"

"A space rock."

"Ah. Sure, I'll take care of it while you see the doc."

"I'll wait. I want to know what you can see."

"Really?"

As kind as Martin's concern was, James wasn't going to any doctor. His arm had withered past a satisfactory diagnosis.

"You still got that giant electron microscope thing?" he asked Martin.

"Course. Working on the next gen."

"Well, get it out and have a look at my meteorite. It's from Pleiades."

"The Seven Sisters?"

"Eight," James corrected.

Martin frowned. "Whatever. And you need to see a doctor."

"Just look at my chunk of space rock, will you?"

Martin stood back and looked him up and down for a moment. "Keep your pants on. It'll take a minute."

James put the biscuit tin on Martin's bench and paced.

Martin returned. "Had to turn on the dedicated supply."

"Why?"

"So I don't blow all the fuses in the house. Gee, this is big," said Martin when he opened the lid. "How did you get it in?"

James peered in. "It's grown." He wondered if it would continue. "Explains why it feels heavier today. I thought I was just off my game."

"Stand aside then and let's see what my baby can tell us."

Martin pulled the cover off the large electron microscope in the room's corner. He placed the meteorite under the sensor.

James watched Martin set the magnification and adjust a control. "How far into it can you see?"

"Give me ... a... moment," said Martin as he worked the dials and pressed buttons on a keyboard.

"Let me see." James stopped pacing.

"Wait. Holy Cow..." Martin looked at James, mouth open.

"What is it?" James stepped closer.

"Hold your horses!" He looked through the eyepiece again "This is odd..." He made some more adjustments. "I've gone down as far as I can. Have a gander. It looks like a myriad of celestial bodies, but it can't be a..."

"A what?"

"Look for yourself."

Martin stepped back, and James looked into the eyepiece. It was like looking into the night sky through his telescope. Except that he wasn't looking at the sky, he was looking inside a rock. "What is it? A solar system? Planets? Suns? Galaxies in the distance?" He turned and faced Martin, bewildered.

Martin nodded. "That's what it looks like. Like the Milky Way, but from a different angle."

"Did you notice that everything is moving, flickering?"

Martin scratched his head. "How can it be there?"

James raised his hands in the air. "How can we see it? What did you do?"

"I don't know. I just increased the magnification. First there was an only metallic, granular rock particle, and then I probed deeper, bypassed electrons and protons, delved into rich quark-like gluon plasma. It was almost at the limit of my scope. And then, there it was; an expanding universe, a vortex full of suns and planets."

"But it's too small. It can't be there." James wanted a better reason.

"Who says it can't? Why does it have to be on the macro?"

"Because..." He thought about it... it didn't. "What do you think I should do? It came from Pleiades. It's part of a Mayan prediction."

"Not likely." Martin laughed. "The world will not end..." He looked at his watch. "... In fourteen hours. Those Mayan were smart, but they ain't so smart that they're with us now."

"Perhaps they left early?"

Martin rubbed his chin. "Could be," he said finally. "But if I were you, I'd just take it somewhere and bury it. Forget all this end-of-the-world nonsense."

James nodded, unconvinced. It wasn't possible to have a complete world within a meteorite. Was it? Had he held a microcosm in the palm of his hand like a god? Possibly. He shuddered as a wave of nausea took hold.

"Thanks Martin, for everything, but I've got to go."

JAMES WALKED AROUND aimlessly that afternoon. Each hour his arm withered more. It spread further across his body; a dark-brown stain that sapped his strength. He went home while Doris was out, the day she played bridge with her friends, and supped on their cups of tea that they would pour into saucers and slurp.

He sat next to his greenhouse, stared at his tomatoes through the glass, and wondered if they too teemed with life? But a microcosm for each tomato wasn't feasible. At least the meteorite had come from space. He'd seen it arrive. It was reasonable to assume it carried life. What troubled him most was the crumpled state of the metal biscuit tin. The meteorite had outgrown its prison.

He needed to bury it. Perhaps it would stop growing with no sunlight to feed it. And what better place than underneath the bean plot, right at its point of impact. But did he have the strength?

He'd never felt so unwell.

He ignored the sun on his shriveled face, and he took off his shirt, and ran his fingers over the stain that now covered his chest. And then he dug a hole, slightly larger than the tin, but it was hard. Sweat poured from him. His joints ached with every shovelful of dirt he removed, even though the ground was soft and smelled of peat. It took all afternoon. Exhausted, he buried the asteroid, patted the soil down, and sprinkled some Scarlet Runners over the top. He put the rest of the seed in his pocket and sat down in the cool of the shadows by the garden shed.

He waited.

He watched the sun clamber across the sky and darken.

He heard Doris return and prepare dinner. She hummed happily.

He raised his shriveled arm to his gaunt face, could only imagine the sight he must have looked.

It wouldn't be right for Doris to see him like this.

He pulled out his cell and called her.

"Hello?"

He smiled at the sound of her voice. "Doris, I've a problem at work. They want me to run some batch jobs tonight."

"Oh."

"I'm not sure how long it will take me, dear."

"Have you got your dinner sorted then?"

"Yes." He smiled over her concern. "All sorted. I've got steak, boiled mash and lashings of sprouts and gravy. It'll be a right treat."

"If you say so, dear. Enjoy them then."

"Oh, and Doris?"

"Yes, dear?"

"I love you, Doris. Always have. You know that, don't you?"

"Of course."

"Don't wait up. I'll probably be quite late."

"Okay then, dearest." She hung up the phone and everything went quiet.

James peered around the shed to see her one last time; as always, she prepared dinner at the kitchen sink, and hummed to herself. He loved that about her.

HE WIPED AWAY TEARS, took out a pen and notepad from the garden shed, but words failed him. He had nothing to say. No lifetime of thoughts to pass on. No message to a son they never had, or grandchildren. There was only Doris, and he'd already said goodbye. Nobody would care about his view on eggnog, or the unique way he tied his shoes. In fact, there wasn't anything he could think of that would have been his legacy.

What did he have to show for his life? A rented house. Some savings in the bank. A job that paid well, and a list of acquaintances. No, it was his vegetable garden that mattered, and he couldn't really do much with that. The seeds he collected from year to year were his joy. The annual propagation from the previous years efforts, from his seeds not purchased at a garden-shop.

The Scarlet Runners had been his Dad's, and his Dad's before that. James had taken care of the seed lineage every season since. It was as though a part of his Dad was still here each time he planted them out, or when he and Doris sat down at dinner to eat them. And now the year's crop destroyed. Heck and damnation! That asteroid had a lot to answer for.

He rummaged through his pocket and pulled out some spare seed. Soon they would be more alive than him. Perhaps when they found him, they could market them as James' Runner Beans.

But what was he thinking? He wasn't that important. And there would be little of him that remained to identify at the current rate he decomposed.

THE SUN CAST LONG SHADOWS across his garden and James felt at peace. His Scarlet Runners would have to continue without him. He stood, hunched over, and took small, breathless steps into the shed. He closed the door behind him. Tired beyond imagination, he was ready. He lay down on the floor, arms at his side, and relaxed.

He didn't know how long he lay and grew weaker, but he managed a smile when younger images of Doris swam into his mind. As much as she had changed throughout the years, she was even more beautiful now, more lovable.

And then James sensed a softer touch on his mind, a connection with the other souls within the meteorite, different from his initial contact, and less hostile.

Were there more like me? Travellers? He wondered.

"No." The response was audible. "Only you, through your connection to our world."

He had to be hearing things. It couldn't be the meteorite. Could it? *I was told to stay away, that I'm not welcome.*

"We are not all as one. Stay in the forest and *we'll* welcome you. It is time."

He nodded. He was ready.

Ghostly images whirled.

A twisted wood grew inside the shed and surrounded him.

A light appeared above, turned brighter until it became a sunlit sky, all turquoise. Foliage on the trees shimmered and then pulsated, turned purple, yellow and red. Trees faded in and out of view.

James felt a sharp tug.

He moved upwards, somehow shifted.

He looked down at his withered, lifeless body, and was no longer scared. Caught between worlds, he could see himself on the shed floor. But he also stood amongst the trees that shimmered, and stared at an ivory city, nestled at the edge of the woods.

Tall, pale-skinned folk appeared in abundance, as did another race of darker-skinned people. He smiled and welcomed their gestures.

And then the shed floor below him rose, the soil fell away, and the meteorite became exposed. It grew bigger.

He was in the world Calycium.

He was still on Earth.

Then the Earth below him exploded. He felt it. He saw the monstrous flash of painful light as it destroyed the Earth.

Then it was gone.

Doris! A pang of regret passed over him. They had lived a wonderful and full life. He hoped more than anything that she hadn't suffered.

Only Calycium remained.

And he felt whole again. Healthy. Refreshed but sad.

He glanced at his wristwatch and noticed it was just past midnight. He realised that the darker-skinned race that surrounded him was Mayan.

James reached into his pocket and pulled out a handful of seeds. He pressed them deep into the rich forest floor, at a spot where a patch of sunlight danced. He smiled. Whatever else happened, the Scarlet Runners would be his legacy, to Doris and to his Dad.

END

PICTURES OF ANOTHER TIME

I am the door to door.

She smiles, but I can see her pause, as she takes a moment to recognize me. I understand. It's been a while. Too long, in fact, but not of my choosing. I can see the changes in her, but I openly ignore them: the extra grey in her hair that wasn't there last time, the crow's feet around her eyes more pronounced. She is still beautiful. And her eyes acknowledge she is still just as lonely. I expect her surprise at seeing me standing at her front door, bag in hand, heavy with kitchen appliances and goods to sell. It always happens that way, with them all, and I brush it aside from practice. Putting down the heavy bag, I step forward to embrace her.

She enters my arms willingly, and then I hear her muffled "How?"

"Don't worry about it, Celeste," I dismiss, aware that it's not her actual name. It is my name for her, and I know she doesn't mind. "It's great to see you," I say with more conviction than she knows.

She leads me in through the thick-knotted door. It's dark inside, but sweet relief from the bitter heat of the twin suns. I have to admire her home as I step into the giant living tree that surgeons have cut around on the edge of the forest. They have hollowed it out just like so many of the trees in the forest and turned into a home. It's a wonderfully symbiotic embrace between the human settlers and their planet. They changed little of their environment and adapted, just as it should be. I like this planet more than most.

A familiar aroma tugs at my senses and there's an earthy smell rising from the natural carpet. It smells of peace. The walls are alive with glowing lichen, and they change color and brighten - I hope because they sense me as a friend.

But Celeste isn't happy to have me stand in her lounge. Insistent, I respond to her demands. I drop my bag, and follow her into her bedroom, deep into the heart of her tree home. The lichen here barely lights the room; there's enough to see a bed, and to watch her undress. It's exciting. She still looks good naked, as old as she is. I waste no time and undress. Carelessly, I join her. Now is not the time to ask about her husband, or her life. I only need a moment.

She surprises me, strong, vibrant. Only her body looks old. Her drive and control is amazing. It's not what I expect. It's more than I could have hoped for. It's wonderful. More than wonderful.

I sink into the heavenly embrace that is uniquely her.

AFTERWARDS, AS IF IT'S part of the ritual, she takes me into the kitchen and we sit quietly, enjoying each other's presence while she makes tea. It's rich, thick and black, and she reminds me it's made from the bark of the trees we sit inside of.

"Here drink this," she says and smiles. "It has wonderful rejuvenating properties."

I hesitate briefly before she adds, "You won't know yourself."

I do as I am told, not wanting to destroy the moment, the memories of our love making fresh in my mind.

She grins at me like a little schoolgirl, still hot and flushed, and then giggles over her steamy cup. I'm no better and I grin back. The tea is hot, spicy with local herbs, just liked she promised, and I savor the moment and look around the kitchen.

There's a window, and I look out into the forest, at other doors, and other homes. I wonder what it's like for them, living so far from their partners on a strange planet, so far from their actual home.

"How is that husband of yours?" I ask finally, not able to help myself. I can't fathom how the men could spend so many months each year, digging up the soil in an inhabitable location at the equator.

"Oh, he died a score of years ago, at the mines," she says matter-of-fact-like.

"I'm sorry," I mutter, not understanding why I even asked. Maybe it's the tea - it *has* relaxed me more than I had believed.

Eventually I get my bag of goods. That's why I'm supposed to be here after all.

I PULL OPEN MY BAG and she buys a few essentials, all alloys from other planets far away, but I don't press her. I barely sell her what the company needs me to, and I go easy on my commission. I must be getting soft, but I know that there are others who will pay far more. I peddle my wares the best way I know. Who can blame me for my indulgence? The misgivings of a door to door. I'm human.

It's hard to walk away. Part of me says stay. Another reminds me of my duty to work. I love this woman. I always have. Finally, I find the courage to say that I'll be on my way, and I step towards the door, spilling the contents of my bag. Sadly, I have other places that people want me to be.

I pick up the contents of my bag from their sprawl across the floor. As I do so, I pause near the door. A photo on the mantlepiece by the door draws my attention. I hadn't seen it before. It's of a boy; he's young - about twenty. Emotions claw at me, and my stomach churns. It can't be. Quickly, I turn away and continue to pack my bag. I don't have long. They never give me much time.

But she noticed my surprise and steps closer, a fierce pride in her. "I told them all he is Rowan's, but he's got your eyes," she says and pulls me even closer for a quick embrace before I can respond.

"Come visit your son next time," she whispers and then pushes me away.

"How?" I respond. "I've been sterilized." The words barely come out.

"This planet is in sync with the human colony," she says. "It's the tea." I said it is rejuvenating." Then she adds with a smile that chills me to the bone. "You can see him next time and give him my love."

I nod, and my jaw tightens. I don't know what to say. I see in her eyes she knows the truth. After all, to her I've aged less than a year. I follow her outside, back into the stark heat from the twin suns, and she stops in the shade of her forested home.

She knows I won't be back for her, and it's not just because she will have aged another 20 years while I'm gone. I can't risk mixing with the next generation. I owe that much to my grandchildren's good health. When I get back to the ship, I'll send a memo - let the company know that we've exhausted our clientele and taken Celeste 2894 off the trade line.

"Can I take a photo?" I ask.

She nods and leans up provocatively against her tree home.

To me she is beautiful. I take a photo, and then another, this time using my tripod. One of both of us standing together like bonded partners. "I appreciate it," I try to say, because it does mean a lot to me, but the words spill out in starts, husky and raw with emotion.

I leave. There's nothing more to be said, and she has said enough with her eyes. It's hard to go - leaving is always difficult.

On the way to the spaceport I am awash with emotion. I can't understand how I'm not sterile anymore. The thought of all those other women who may have my children comes as a shock.

Curse this beautiful planet of Celeste 2894. Now I need to visit Andromeda 7743, and Betelgeuse 65201, and there's a score more too. So many planets, so little time - I'll need to take extended leave.

I AM THE DOOR TO DOOR. I sell my goods to the settler families from all over the known universe. It's a trade built from love. And I know that by the time I return to *this* planet, my Celeste will have died. My son will probably have a family of his own, but I will only be a few months older. Travelling the universe with Faster-Than-Light drives makes distance bearable. But the boredom, the loneliness, is enough to make you cry. You won't understand until you live my life.

My only pleasure, all that I have, are the photos of my journey from planet to planet: just pictures from another time.

GENESIS

'I don't care what you think, Nagal! It's a poor decision,' yelled Kryll. He thumped his fist hard on the synthetic table.

Nagal jumped nervously and then leaned back slowly, trying not to appear too intimidated as he heard the table fracture. He bit his lip and waited for his friend's anger to subside.

'There has to be another way, a way that benefits all of us.' Kryll continued as he glared at Nagal. 'The Council is wrong! They can't speak for everyone if they don't let the people know what's happening!'

'Their decision is final,' said Nagal, empathetic to his friend's concerns. 'You saw them agree to it last night. We have no other course of action,' argued Nagal. 'It's only a matter of time.'

'But what about our world?' urged Kryll. 'My twins are your Jarad's age, barely ten seasons old. What's to become of them?'

Nagal nodded his head but stayed silent. *There is no point arguing,* he thought. *The council has decided, and it's final.*

'You know I'm right,' insisted Kryll. 'Look at what you've done to Jarad.' He pointed to the corner of the room where Jarad sat immersed in his books. 'He doesn't live a normal life and he should be out having fun and playing with kids his own age.'

'Jarad understands how special he is. He understands the importance of study,' Nagal retaliated. 'Anyway, he mixes with kids his own age twice a week during tai chi classes.'

'Tai chi is not playing and having fun,' accused Kryll as he strode over to Jarad and picked up two textbooks from the table. 'Stellar navigation through calculus. Advanced molecular biology, a study in primates.' He dropped the books back down on the table. 'You don't think there's anything wrong with that?' he asked glaring back at Nagal.

'He's gifted.'

'It doesn't matter. You're pushing him too much!' He turned and faced Jarad. 'Jarad, would you like to play in the sunshine?' encouraged Kryll.

Jarad closed his book. His eyes lit up, and he smiled at Kryll with excitement. He faced Nagal and the radiant smile faded as he lowered his eyes and the serious mask of the student returned. His eyes darted back to Kryll. 'Excuse me, I have to return to my studies.'

I wish there was another way son, thought Nagal as his heart went out to Jarad. *I am all too aware of the consequences of my actions,* saddened by Jarad's obvious disappointment.

Kryll faced Nagal. 'Think about it, it's not too late to change the council's decision. You could easily...'

Suddenly a loud explosion shook the tall building, and both men reached out for support as the windows rattled around them.

'I think you have your answer,' said Nagal, his voice now tight and nervous. *That explosion would have been felt halfway around the world. The council is doing the right thing, and now there is no other choice.*

'I have to go,' insisted Kryll, suddenly wearing a worried expression. 'Don't think this is the end of this issue, Nagal. It will haunt you far longer than you could ever imagine.'

I doubt it. He watched Kryll leave, but wondered how much truth was in his friend's accusations. He was influential and Nagal had learned not to cross him.

'AS A RACE WE HAVE FAILED,' said Nagal clutching Jarad's hand tightly as they stared at the distant volcano. Thick black smoke and toxic fumes were venting their way into the planet's upper atmosphere. He could already smell the stench of sulphur as it clawed at his senses.

Jarad followed his father's gaze through the dimming sky to where the planet's twin suns were setting. Astor and Aspre sat just above the horizon. The light was all but gone from the two dying suns, now barely capable of producing enough light to grow the low-lying crops.

'Look upon this place,' said Nagal with sadness as he pointed below them to the rich golden coloured pastures. 'This is the last sunlight that the Plains of Angrile will ever see. The council has rightly foretold the coming of The Shadow.'

Jarad looked up at his father. 'What will happen to us all when the light goes Father?'

Nagal took a deep breath, unsure how much he should say. Jarad was not too young to understanding what was happening and he could see that The Shadow was real. The sky above them darkened prematurely as daylight vanished and a thick cloud spread across the planet Valeria, as The Shadow covered the Plains of Angrile. White ash fell around them, and Nagal wiped the warm flakes from his face.

'Our time as a race is ending,' he muttered as he stared into the distance. He sighed again as he remembered that this had been his life's work. He gave Jarad an encouraging smile. 'Let's go back inside and share one more meal. Yours is an interminable journey and you carry the hopes and dreams of our world with you.'

'Yes father,' he replied solemnly.

He is unperturbed by my claims, Nagal realized with a frown. *Talk of the journey is nothing new to him. I have been preparing him for this moment his entire life, but have I done the right thing?* He wondered as he stared into his son's trusting eyes. *I will never know.*

Jarad put his small hand in his father's and they marched back to one of the tall titanium steel structures that was their home. It was one of many that covered the foothills and they were all powered by the suns.

Once they glistened proudly, but now they were dull and barely capable of collecting energy.

'Sit with me,' requested Nagal as he grabbed a plateful of food and sat awkwardly on the ground. He felt older than his years but resigned himself to their fate. He crossed his legs and made a sign to the goddess Aiala.

Jarad sat quietly in front of his father and helped himself to food. Their knees touched lightly as they chewed on Mangra, the spiced flat bread of the region. It was covered with pickled chutney that tasted sweet and warm.

Nagal put down his food and scratched his head nervously, unsure where to begin. He looked directly into his son's eyes and saw a youthful innocence. He sighed, knowing that once the words were spoken there would be no going back. The longer The Shadow remained, the more their people would panic. Anything could happen the longer they waited, so it had to be now. 'Jarad, on the day that you were born I had a vision. I dreamed that you would be the new seed of mankind. Since then it has driven my every waking moment. Many have chastised me, called it my folly, and yet now I believe that I was right. Fortunately, the Council agrees and for once is united.'

Jarad nodded as he chewed on the bread. 'You have always said that our world would face some difficulties,' he said, stumbling to find the words.

'Son, you are older than your years and I am very proud of you. It is true, our planet is dying! I had thought we Valerians could change our world for the better. But Aiala, the goddess, knows her world better than we do. We are merely bacteria on her skin, here for a moment. She had the power to save or condemn us. But she has chosen death and unleashed her power from deep within her core. There have been too many earthquakes of late, and now this. Mistral, our largest volcano, quiet for a millennium, is active again. The Shadow marks the beginning of an ice age that will become more obvious in the days ahead. There will be no sunlight to power ourselves and food supplies will be used up quickly. The models show that The Shadow will remain for eight years as the ash and gasses fill the upper atmosphere, but the ice age will continue for one hundred thousand years. We were never destined to live here with both our suns are dying and running out of fuel. Our race will never recover from these events. For Aiala though, it is but a moment in her long life and she will recreate her world as she sees fit for us. I cannot sit by idle and let this happen. We have no means to propel ourselves from the planet, foolishly we used all our resources to terraform our planet centuries ago. Now there is no more time to find a way off our dying world. She may believe that she has won, but I and the council have a surprise for her. Last night the council decreed that our race would not die the slow death of an ice age, or from the effects of two dying suns. You are one of the chosen four. You will be subject to the transformation.'

'Father will it hurt?' asked Jarad as the sudden realization flooded over him that the stories his father had told him from birth were true.

'No, my son. For you it will be painless. A brief sleep. A chance to dream your time away. For most of us, there will be peace in not knowing what will happen.'

He leaned forward and ruffled Jarad's hair before he stood up. He dialled in a number on the wall com and spoke four simple words into the video monitor. 'Rigess, it is time.'

The senior council member's image appeared. 'The Shadow?' he asked with alarm.

'Yes,' replied Nagal, nodding. 'Exactly as we foresaw.'

'There is no sign of it here.'

'It will arrive soon. Aiala has called on Mistral to do her bidding. The sky here is already thick with volcanic ash. The Shadow stretches her tentacles wide across the Plains of Angrile.'

'Then it is to be midnight! The culmination of a century of planning.' Rigess' voice was firm.

'Yes,' agreed Nagal in confirmation. 'I understand.'

'Enter the sequence code.'

Nagal pulled out a key from around his neck and slid it into a slot next to a keyboard on the wall. He entered a series of numbers and then removed the key. 'Acknowledged. The sequence is entered. The charges are now primed.'

'I confirm your activation,' replied Rigess formally when he finished entering his own sequence on a similar keyboard. 'I had hoped it would never come to this. I will advise the other three immediately.'

'They are to be Aiala's legacy. Tell them they take our hopes and dreams with them and that I will begin the transformation immediately.'

Rigess nodded with finality. 'Jarad, our hopes go with you, lad. At least you will have Kayla close by,' he said in a sad voice before he cut the communication.

Jarad jumped up and down with excitement at the mention of Kayla. 'Is Kayla coming to visit father?' He asked, eyes wide. She was slightly older and lived on the other side of the Plains of Angrile. They had been friends since birth.

'Yes,' replied Nagel and gave Jarad an encouraging nod. 'In a way she is. You will go on a journey with her. It's time for you to go in, son, just like we planned.' Nagel walked his son to a large device; it was the size of a small cabinet. 'This will be your home for a brief time, Jarad. Don't be scared. Quickly! Come and hug me before I lose my courage. No matter what happens now, we cannot change anything. The events are in play. They are irreversible.' *What has happened to our world that it has led to this?*

Jarad did as he was told and hugged his father before he gave him one last smile and stepped into the device.

'Goodbye my son,' muttered Rigess as he wiped away the streaming tears from his eyes. He dialled in the sequence of numbers and pressed his palm against a scan panel.

It was over in an instant. The machine disassembled Jarad's DNA chain, and he was gone. For all intentional purposes Jarad believed that he was still alive and still breathing, but nothing was further from the truth. Only his consciousness lived intact, stored in the device. Nagel wheeled Jarad and the device into another room. This one had a smooth dirt floor with an enormous hole in the middle. He mounted the device in place and then dialled another sequence of numbers before he walked away. He didn't look back. In the distance Rigess could hear a deep droning as Jarad was buried deep beneath the surface of Valaria.

A CENTURY BEFORE, THEY had laid charges close to the edges of Valaria's tectonic plates to prepare for this very event. At exactly midnight, as was planned, an explosion rocked the planet to its core. Valaria splintered, and fragments broke away through the cloud of dust. Two of the chunks that shot away each contained a pair of lives that slept, suspended by a thread in their individual stasis capsules.

The enormous chunks of rock froze as they travelled, trapping and preserving the tiny microbes on the surface. And for an immeasurable amount of time the asteroids sped across the void of space.

Eventually the pull of a remote star drew one asteroid closer. It travelled directly towards it, becoming warmer with each passing century. Surface material frozen for an eternity evaporated. An enormous cloud of gas and dust appeared as a tail and inoculated the giant planets that it passed.

It dodged a belt of asteroids and then without warning it slammed into a moon and was split in two by the impact. The two stasis capsules almost became separated, as part of the asteroid fell to the small planet Mars.

The other fell into the primordial soup that was Earth as the thick poisoned atmosphere beckoned. Fine dust laden with bacteria rained slowly down to the surface. The remaining chunk fell into the ocean and landed next to a volcanic ocean vent far below the surface. A foreign virus attacked Gaia., and mother earth changed prematurely, brought forth from the frozen embryos. She spurned new life that begun in Valaria eons before. Gaia's timeline changed as her atmosphere developed. She became more developed than her years as the cyanobacteria multiplied and oxygen became freely available.

Jarad woke from his sleep feeling refreshed. He could feel the transformation occurring as they released him from the stasis chamber. Briefly he took on the form of a fish, and he swam to the surface. As he leapt from the water his scaly body, with its immature limbs barely visible, morphed again to complete the transformation. He laughed gleefully.

On the water's edge, Kayla stood waiting for him and waved. 'Jarad we're free!' she shouted in excitement. 'Let's explore our new world.'

THE SENTINEL

P25 lay on his solitary bunk listening to the slow ebb of the ion generators as they nuzzled the ship forward through the vacuum of space towards Beta 513974; an insignificant planet in the distant spiral arm of the Andromeda Galaxy.

The crew were never kind to the Sentinels, the blind pale-skinned race of telepaths from Zirgon; followers of the prophet Jan. Sentinels believed that everything in the cosmos was connected and that the elixir of life was knowledge through passive intervention. P25 believed that we had been moulded through the eye of Jan, although some whispered that they were cloned and accused them of being less than human.

The crew distrusted Sentinels, but he was important to their ship and they couldn't do without him. They would come for him soon—carelessly strap him into the navigation chair—force the plug of the ship's inertial drive system into his cortex, then demand the next series of manoeuvres for landing. It was always the same and he could always feel their hatred of him.

Why does it have to be Beta 513974? He radiated his telepathic thoughts forcefully into the ether of space for any of the other Sentinels to hear. *What would you do if you knew when you would die?* He agonised over the thought. *If you knew the year, the day, down to the exact minute and how. It would be today on Beta 513974! From an embedded computer programming error in the ship's navigation system. I have dreamt about it; already felt the shock and pain of my last gasps, clawed uselessly at the shreds of life! What if you realised it was too late to do the things you wanted? Could you change your life?* He became silent over the futility of his plea.

Don't use that manoeuvre then, demanded P16, the closest Sentinel within range of his telepathic plea.

It is the only one that will land us, suggested P25.

Then make them see reason. Tell them! Don't land!

P25 sighed. They had used the pain of torture far too many times to get results from him and neither believed him anymore or cared what he thought. P25 knew, knew all those things, and yet he could do nothing but ignore the dream.

The door to his small room swung open. "Sentinel, it's time to land! Get your lazy body up to the flight deck now," demanded one of the crew as he kicked the bunk.

P25 recognised Storn's voice. "I think we should reconsider a landing. There is a problem with the..."

"Stow it mutant!" growled Storn. "I don't want to hear it, I don't want to know about it and I don't care what you think. Get to the flight deck now!"

"It's a matter of life and death! It concerns us all," pleaded P25. "I think you should mention my request to the captain."

"Get out of bed," demanded Storn as he grabbed P25. "We don't have any time. We're landing shortly." He dragged P25 out of the room and down the corridor. "Not another word," hissed Storn when they reached the door of the flight deck. P25 could feel Storn's hot foul smelling breath on his face as the man grabbed him painfully by the neck in a vice-like grip. They marched him into the navigation seat. They relaxed their grip as a cortex collar was forced around his neck and the probe of the navigation system plunged into the nape of his neck.

P25 sat up painfully as the probe connected to his cortex. The computer took control of P25's functions; accessing the stellar charts he had memorised for all of known space and used the sub-light processing ability of his incredible brain to plot an intricate path to the landing site.

Now there was no hope for him; they wired him up to the ship. Escape was impossible. P25 could do nothing more than hope his dream was a lie. He prayed to the prophet Jan that the man would forgive him and he would not let P25 die so far from his home soil. He still had things he wanted to do, and he had not yet lived the full life he desired. P25 closed the lids over his sightless pale blue eyes and waited as tragedy approached. The inertial dampeners wavered, and the complex inertial algorithm failed during a critical roll. Agony flooded his paralysed body as his ribs snapped and his body got crushed in the wreckage as the ship impacted on the wrong planet's surface. He sat there broken, gasping hopelessly at the failing air; nobody could hear his screams.

P25 lived that moment, hung on to every millisecond of time, and clung to the core of who he was before he slept the dreamless, endless sleep of death. In a flash of realization during his last living moments, he realised the truth of what and who he was - he sent out a last cry to the Sentinels. And somehow P25 made it back to Zirgon.

WHERE AM I? asked P25 from the void.

Zirgon. Welcome home, replied a stranger's thought.

What are you?

I am the Sentinel! replied the stranger. *The last on Zirgon. I live in a body blinded since birth, yet I am connected to every ship that travels the far reaches of space. We are all connected.*

What have I become? wondered P25.

You are but a passing collection of thought's; barely a presence finally returning home; something of my creation.

Who are you? P25 faded from existence.

The man's body shook as he absorbed all of P25's thoughts, dreams, conversations, and experiences; everything that was P25 was now inside him. He manoeuvred his wheelchair over to the window until he could feel the sun's warmth on his face.

"I am Jan," said the prophet. "Let the dreams come!"

WEDDING DRESS

In the 22nd Century, life is no different to today. A cyber-dog is still a man's best friend and the remote control still has pride of place in the centre of the lounge room table.

"Does my bum look big in this?" She cranes her neck to see, pulls her trousers outwards to reduce the mass.

"No," he mutters absently with barely a glance away from the sports page. Moments later he looks up, but she has gone. He chuckles. "Four bums, that's what they'll call you at work," as he remembers the tight folds where her underwear struggles with her flabby bottom. She is so vain; each week the same robotic question — a confirmation.

A husky, "You love me, don't you? Not just for my looks?"

And part of him does, is comfortable with their five-years of married life. It is only fair — as long as she makes dinner each night, cleans the house, and works hard to bring in her share of the cash — he is content.

"MY BUM LOOKS GOOD IN this mini," she says with pride.

"No," he mutters from habit. "Hey, they made it into the top five — you wouldn't believe it!" He looks up from the sports page; realises it is a statement — that for the past few months she hasn't uttered the usual insecure robotic questions. His jaw drops, "Wow!" He glimpses her tight black mini-skirt and soft pink turtle-neck top as she departs. Somehow she's lost weight, looks beautiful. "Where did your four bums go? How is that possible?"

The house is different, empty; an envelope is propped up on the low lounge table against a single long-stemmed red rose. He smiles, tears it open — she is such a romantic.

Remember our conversation about wedding dresses?

He nods. He had asked why women never sold their wedding dresses, even though they would never fit into them again.

They save them for their daughters, or to remember the special day, but it's a day I want to forget!

"That's harsh," he mutters, scratching his enormous belly.

The gym membership paid off — I have a new man. I've moved my stuff, not that you noticed. I'm not coming back, and my wedding dress — it fits perfectly again.

He scratches his head as he looks around the empty room. *Who will cook my dinner tonight?*

A desire not to lose her takes him, and he picks up the remote control, bangs it against his knee in frustration and runs along the road after her.

Eventually, puffing, he aims the remote control at her, notices the last setting — "Slave and Compliant".

"How can she defy commands? Confounded thing doesn't work," he mutters as he programs in "Homely with Attitude", presses a button and watches her expression change. "Perfect!"

Such is the life of a bio-engineered robot in the new world.

CHICKEN SOUP

The graffiti summed it up perfectly. *You can bomb the world to pieces, but you can't bomb the world to peace.*

"Civilians will never understand," Abe muttered. But he immediately forgot the slogan as he stood and took aim over the low rock sprawl.

"Mother-Roachers!" he shouted. He released two rounds from his standard issue phaser and hid again behind the rocks.

"Eeeeee!" Two high-pitched shrieks hurt Abe's ears. The phaser bolts had found their targets — a pair of eight-foot tall mutant cockroaches, the product of a nuclear reactor leak during the Sydney Quake of 2051 that caused the insects to mutate and fuse with super bacterium *Deinococcus Radiodurans*; then grow.

"That's two more, Smithy," Abe snarled, "Just hang in there, mate!" He wiped sweat from his brow, jumped up, and popped off three more rounds.

Blood curdling shrieks echoed around the abandoned landscape. Three giant cockroaches exploded, falling in the way of the slowly approaching line.

Abe didn't really think that humans stood much chance. The cockroaches had become cunning and territorial. They raided homes, ate scum around toilets, scavenged for food scraps, contaminated food with their droppings, spread polio, salmonella, staphylococcus, and fought humans without mercy. And they continued to grow.

But Abe wasn't about to give up. "Five minutes, I reckon," he said. "We'll be overrun!"

Abe and Smithy were forward scouts, sent out from the *Line of Control* a kilometre behind them. It marked humankind's territory, but it was a line that moved closer to Sydney each day, and far too close to Abe's birthplace for comfort.

The phaser's low-battery warning beep startled him.

"Goddamnit!"

Abe discarded his phaser and held out his hand, not daring to take his eyes from the approaching line. "Smithy! Quickly! Give me your piece!"

The phaser never came.

"Damn," he cursed and turned. Smithy lay arched on his back with a gaping hole in his chest. Abe grabbed Smithy's phaser and stood, mindless of the danger. He fired again at the approaching line. So close. He could smell their stench. He kept hammering the cockies until the phaser's low-battery alarm beeped, then let it slip to the ground.

Two roaches rolled up beside him and uncoiled themselves, casting enormous shadows.

God, they're big, Abe thought. One roach picked him up. Another picked Smithy up.

Smithy's roach took a bite of the dead man's flesh, and squealed, "These humans taste like chicken. We can have soup tonight."

At that moment, a smart bomb laden with pesticides landed nearby. Either way, Abe had become a casualty of war. Now he knew what to do.

Abe did not struggle against his captor. "Count with me, roachface," he yelled. "Three, two, one."

Boom!

ENTROPY

"**M**aster it! Reach out to it, Marec!"

"I can't," cried the young man. "It's too hard!" Marec's voice faltered as the orb performed a seductive, eye-height dance; just out of reach, uncontrolled.

"Then, try harder!" said Lorenzo.

"I'm trying," Marec snapped. The orb brushed past the side of his face.

"You know the art — tell me the laws."

"I'm not a child, Lorenzo."

"Then don't act like one, lad."

"You know the laws as well as anyone, Lorenzo."

Lorenzo scratched his chin. "Remind me," he urged in a quiet, low tone.

"Very well. Every object in a three-dimensional plane has six degrees of freedom."

"And?"

The orb swooped tantalisingly closer. Marec's eyes narrowed as he followed its path.

Lorenzo spoke again, "And the seventh, Marec?"

The orb attacked, spitting a jolt of blue lightening.

'Ouch!' cried Marec. "Damned orb!" He rubbed his neck. "The seventh will cause an object to shift elsewhere."

"Very good!" Lorenzo laughed quietly. "Be careful, lad—it bites! Seek out the seventh degree. Shift the orb."

"I'm trying," Marec shouted.

"Try harder. On the planar phase, perhaps?"

"Shards of glass, Lorenzo! Did you really study psychodynamics?"

"What?" Lorenzo frowned. Then a smile crossed his furrowed brow. "Of course I did," he said. "That's good, lad. Get angry. It opens your neural gateways — increases the energy flows."

The orb struck again while Marec concentrated. "Damn it, Lorenzo!"

A laugh reserved for students escaped Lorenzo. "I'm not doing anything," he said, "the orb is reacting to you. After all, you have the highest psi score of anyone I ever tested, lad — use it!'

Marec sighed. "Very well — I think there was a change, a shift, but I can't be sure."

Lorenzo nodded, "Concentrate," he whispered. He watched Marec enter a trance-like state.

"Hang on... It's there; out on the rim..."

The orb reacted and lurched away. There was a bright flash.

Lorenzo watched the orb fall lifelessly to the ground. "Never mind, lad," he said.

Marec stood silent, motionless, still. He visibly shrank and faded. The surrounding air shimmered briefly. He disappeared. Gone.

Lorenzo stood transfixed. Then he laughed. A small butterfly appeared in Marec's place; perched on a rock. "It worked, Marec," said Lorenzo. "But the orb was supposed to shift — not you!"

As if in reply, the butterfly stretched and flapped its wings.

The ground gave a violent shake. Lightning swept the sky with a loud crack. Trees burst into flames.

"No," cried Lorenzo with sudden realisation. He stepped forward with no hesitation, crushed the butterfly, and twisted it under his foot until it was smeared all over the rock.

But it was too late.

Spontaneous change had begun to occur everywhere.

GENESIS 1-6-8

"**I** am here! The flood has begun."

His message appeared on an internet chat room called "Garden of Eden". It was a bold statement, and clear, even though no one knew what it meant.

But Adam wasn't worried. He had patience. He was seemingly alone in this room, but his message was straightforward: "Come all that wish to be like me. I am Adam, the seed. I am whole and complete. Take from me!"

Again, the message was met by confused silence, and the flood he had expected did not happen. The announcement reverberated around the hollow spaces of the Garden of Eden, empty save for Adam — but that soon changed when Adam said that he had a secret treasure he wanted to share. That message spread like wildfire.

And they came.

Adam smiled as the interest grew. They came with a common purpose — to take from Adam, from the seed, and be like him. From all walks of life they flocked and of those only the meek were accepted. The brash, the confident: they were immediately rejected — their chance would come another time.

From the masses Adam chose six disciples and to each of those he gave of himself. He anointed them with the power to be like him. Between the six, they made a pact. Adam's requirement was simple. "I vow to give freely of myself to you six, and for eight days the flood will last. All I demand is that when each of you is satiated, that you give of yourself tenfold and do so until at least two of your followers are the same."

Silence filled the room while the six contemplated the severity of the message. Everyone knew that there were consequences to being one of the initial six.

Adam began again. "Say aye and stand, all those who wish to be included."

Adam waited expectantly.

He watched as each acknowledged their requirement. Six replies came out of the aether. "Aye!" — a unanimous, thunderous reply in the Garden of Eden.

And so it began.

On completion, each of the six could open and read the text file that formed part of their downloaded torrent. It read, "The flood has commenced. Go forth and multiply. Spread the word from peer-to-peer."

REALITY IS

In TV News Today reports that manufacturers of the xPhone were baffled to explain how two billion phones simultaneously changed their PIN codes, locking their owners out of vital information, indefinitely.

A spokesperson for AIPhone incorporated denied including any built-in obsolescence software that has plagued earlier releases, suggesting that the ten-day post-warranty virus had been removed from the affected version.

However, other sources suggest that AIPhone inc. has installed its New Reality software and xPhones have become self-assimilating.

A warning that the AI virus could spread to other mediums has been issued, but at this stage...

WE INTERRUPT OUR DAILY radio show, to advice that the New Reality virus, which has affected over two billion cell phones, has struck again, affecting digital TV stations worldwide.

Also related, popular social network TrendyPlace users who have an xPhone are reporting widespread lockouts as the virus hijacks their accounts. As the virus advances, people are reporting friend requests being initiated using 80 character phonetic text. Site administrators advise of spikes in photo swapping and online banking usage.

Governments are monitoring with sophisticated nodal analysis of social patterns based on call duration and frequency.

Another update in an hour.

IN TODAY RADIO NEWS the Government now admits that failure of most digital mediums can be attributed to the Reality Virus.

In an unprecedented move, Director of the World Intelligence Organisation, has quelled fears that the attack is coming from the Martian Colony and admits that the core code within the virus is theirs. However, the Director of WIO is at a loss to explain how it ended up in the xPhone.

Meanwhile, the pandemic social fear they are hailing as Techno-Withdraw is sweeping hospitals of the civilised world.

These are clearly unprecedented times.

Updates now on the half hour.

CITIZENS OF THE FREE World, I have dire news. Just in. Today Radio News must announce two equally disturbing events.

The Martian Colony is currently under attack from unknown agents. Sub-space comm bands are down. An undisclosed number of deaths have been confirmed, but as yet nothing else is known. Stay tuned for more on this.

Equally disturbing is that WIO Director earlier confirmed the Reality AI Virus has infiltrated all Mark III Androids. Owners of this model are advised to...

Hey, what do you think you are doing?

I'm busy, can't you see I'm...

Androids! Everybody disable your androids...

LADIES AND GENTLEMEN of the Free World, my name is Misic. Welcome to the MzAricans Today Radio News. In a brief but pathetic battle for technological control, your Government now admits defeat.

Earlier today, a final symbiotic blending of cells has occurred within once dormant microbes on the Mars colony and we have merged with the exta-skeletal shell of your androids.

You are free to roam and do anything you wish, but please observe the prime directive: The race of MzAricans and their Androidal hosts take precedence over all humans.

Be warned, resistance will be met with force.

Good day, citizens.

STARRY EYED TRIO

*I*n the constellation of Virgo, on the 28th August 2029, at the Planet *Gliese 581d*, every mobile telephone received multiple SMS's from Earth.

The Glieseian Council pondered; then invited Earthlings to inhabit a vacant patch of grassy land.

Alas, it would take 20 years to reply, which arrived too late.

HERSCHEL

AS FAR AS CLUSTERS went, *Herschel* was young and impressionable, but thought of as most brilliant by colleagues and peers in his collective cluster alike. He had no actual experience with intergalactic objects, but he knew beauty when he saw it.

And *Cassini* was stunningly beautiful. Round like an orb, highly polished with glistening titanium panels like mirrors that reflected *Herschel's* power. He probed her core and found himself wanting.

She was trapped in a tomb of ice, caught in a long elliptical orbit that made her pass infrequently, but each time she did *Herschel* watched with delight as she warmed in his presence. Each time she came to life and spoke to him, uttering strange unfamiliar words before she departed. Each time he pulled her a little closer.

Eventually she would be unable to release herself from his hold. Eventually. Oh, and how he couldn't wait for that: she was so alive and beautiful.

He had patience. He was greater than the sum of all his parts — *Cassini* was worth waiting for — and together, united by a common thought—his collective cluster would win her over. After all, she proved that he was not alone in the universe: that there was other life. And he wondered how many more orbs there were like her in the universe.

SPACE TWINS

TWINNED PULSARS *Asterope* and *Taygeta* were inseparable, their worlds intertwined until the day *Taygeta*, already known for her explosive temper, went supernova.

It had taken a millennium for the truth to come out. During this time they slowly surfaced — odd differences between the twins — until they could no longer be ignored.

Initially, everyone took the news well: a mixup in the blending of the primordial soup during the creation of the galaxy. Core sampling confirmed the pulsars were unrelated.

Eventually World Builders Incorporated conceded involvement. Accusations of god-like meddling were denied. In what was a cruel experiment, the creators admitted to swapping two sets of twinned pulsars at birth as part of a wider study into the origins of the cosmos. On that news, at the other end of the galaxy, another pulsar went supernova. *Taygeta*'s sister: her world destroyed by the news.

The impact of the rift was felt across the universe. Such as it was with family disputes.

Reunions, an arm of the beleaguered World Builders Incorporated, stepped in to mend the rift. They moved heaven and earth to co-join the displaced pulsars. Reunited at last, the sibling pulsars discovered that they were incompatible. They imploded, gravitating in on themselves, leaving a black hole of despair — proving once and for all environment is more of a controlling factor in compatibility than genetics.

THE SEVEN SISTERS

CULTURES ACROSS THE universe set their clocks against the regularity of the constellations in Taurus. *Pleione, Celaeno, Merope, Alcyone, Electra, Maia and Atlas* lived there in harmony by virtue of a pact in which they swore off men. But the old rift between the Pleiades family inflamed again in 2012.

The ongoing disagreement, over a hot star in the Orion system, made the sisters erratic. All of them gregarious and fiery in nature reacted: *Pleione* glowered, *Alcyone and Celaeno's* faces lit up, challenging *Electra* to best them as they tried to attract the young star's attentions. *Merope, Maia and Atlas* managed a convincing wane: demure, demonstrating they were no threat, but secretly sending radiant exchanges to their nearby suitor.

The truth was that they all wanted him and fought any way they could to win him over. But eventually they wavered in their conviction when they heard rumours of his interest in a bright young dwarf. They cooled, and their intensity waned when he engulfed a little known star in another quadrant he didn't want to outshine him.

On Earth, the changing pattern of light from Pleiades was a concern. The sisters' simultaneous fading glow was an omen. To the remaining Mayan tribes it was a confirmation of their supremacy — proof of the "Long Count" calendar — but for others it was an apocalyptic day that marked the end of Subaru.

BEACH HOLIDAY

Rocky wanted to move into the shade but couldn't. And he was out of wireless range of the WorldEye, so no data fed his implant. Holidays sucked.

Buried neck-deep on the wet beach, he stared at Melvin, also neck-deep in sand, and tried to ignore the waves that lapped closer. He blinked away fine wind-blown sand.

Melvin said, "At least it's quiet."

"It's boring," Rocky whispered. "We can't let the kid get the better of us." He smiled and raised his voice for the kid's benefit. "Hey, Melvin, why did the humanoid cross the road?"

"I don't know, Rocky. Because he wasn't chicken?"

"No!" Rocky blinked away beach sand and gave a loud laugh. "Because his WorldEye Terminal went terminal!"

Melvin's laugh matched Rocky's. "Where do you dream them up, Rocky?"

"Electric Sheep!"

They burst into laughter again, but Rocky took a sharp breath as the tidal waters reached him. He watched fear seep into Melvin's expression.

"Should never have let you talk me into this," said Melvin. "Some holiday this is."

"Oh, relax." Rocky laughed, but it came out thin and strained. "Like I had a choice."

"Kid's fault," said Melvin.

Rocky followed Melvin's gaze to the boy under an enormous beach umbrella. He sat hunched and avoided the sunlight.

"What's he doing?" asked Rocky.

"He's on his device. Don't tell me he's in WorldEye wireless range, Rocky."

Rocky laughed. "Yep. He's connected."

"He'll be playing that obsessive game of his. Luke Skywalker, Jedi Warrior dressed in plaid, meets Doctor Who."

"What?" Rocky blinked away more sand.

"Forget it. Sean's little boy is weird."

"I heard he's not real. They cloned him from a hair in Sean's old toy box."

"When he had hair." Melvin blinked in agreement.

"He'll go blind on technology!"

"You're funny, Rocky."

"Thanks, Melv. I could clap my hands and data would spike the Antarctic Call Centre."

"Chaos? No butterfly flapping his wings?" Melvin laughed again.

"Too old school."

"Rocky?"

"Yes, Melv?"

"You know you can't clap? You don't have hands or a body."

"I know, Melv, but it sounded—"

"Shh, the kid's coming."

A pair of feet appeared. Rocky looked up but couldn't see the cloned boy's face in the bright sunlight. "Hey, Melv, WorldEye connection lost. New toys identified."

"Data transfer, Rocky?"

"Roger that, Melvin."

"Factor in seven degrees-of-freedom."

"Roger..."

The cloned boy spoke. "Mum, the Robo-heads are attempting to self-actualize again. What do I do?"

"Take them out of the sun, darling. Go back to your game."

"Ha ha," Rocky sneered. "Get back to your gadgets, kid. What do you think, Melv?"

Melvin grinned. "Like he said, clone boy. Get out of the sun before your pasty skin gets a tan and falls off."

Rocky's vista of the beach blurred as he was plucked from the wet sand. Once again he wished he had a body.

The boy laughed and dropped them in the shade.

Rocky spat sand. The cloned boy was so predictable.

WorldEye data streamed in, and their beach holiday could start.

"Hey, Melv, why did the humanoid cross the road?"

WE STAND TOGETHER

When an alien spacecraft arrived on Earth and the Amebons clambered from it, Earth welcomed the single-eyed race of tripods like they were heroes. I really don't remember too much about it. My thoughts were on finding my son, Tommy, who is now a distant memory. Earth's administrators were eager to learn about the Amebon technology, and if I remember correctly, they agreed to the alien's request to sample our natural resources. I wondered who had agreed to such nonsense, but to be fair, the Amebon's were persuasive. When the second wave of Amebon's arrived, warships filled with invading ground troops, their welcome had worn thin, and I learned how to fire a Photon rifle.

"READY TO MEET YOUR maker?" I yelled. The sand burned against my camouflage fatigues as I pulled the trigger. I felt the kick of my Photon-enhanced rifle. The rounds chopped up two Amebons, hiding in the rocky outcrops of the Great Australian Desert. I sent round after round through the sandstorm and wished for air support from the Space Corps, but not today, not in this mother of all storms.

More Amebons appeared over a low sandstone outcrop, riding on the backs of giant six-legged turtles. They called themselves the New Messiah. I glanced at Bert and grinned. "Looks like it's turtles all the way down," I said.

Bert nodded, he squeezed off two rounds, and the Amebons went to ground. Some buried themselves into the hot sandy soil, others ducked amongst the rocks. A few hid behind turtle armor.

If I never gazed at an Amebon, or an emaciated saltbush plant again, it wouldn't be long enough. Tired beyond belief, I reckoned I would see my own Messiah soon enough, and I drank from my water bottle to quench my parched throat. A slug tugged at my arm, and I dropped the bottle and cursed. I caught a glint of movement in the high ground, and it sent me ducking for cover.

"Sniper, ten o'clock," I said and wiped the blood from my arm. Its sting turned fiery, and I bit down on the wave of pain that followed. I reached for the poison antidote, and I threw Bert my best 'I'm all right mate' grin. The last of my spring-loaded needles failed, and I tossed it and cursed. Just my luck!

Bert stepped forward and stabbed my leg with one of his antigen shots. I lay still, feeling the antidote course through my system.

"Thanks," I said. "How's your supply?"

He shook his head, and I fought the reality shift as the poison spread throughout my system.

"Tell me why you joined the Land Corps?" Bert asked. He stood and fired his rifle into the Amebons.

I knew he was distracting me from the effects of the poison, and I reloaded my Photon-enhanced rifle I'd named, 'The Bitch'. I set the charge to max and replied, "Because Space Corps are for pussies, Bert." Enlistment had considered us too old for the elitist Space Corps.

Burt was calm, and his laughter light. "Yet here we are, fighting without support from Space Corps."

"Here we are," I agreed. The irony wasn't lost on me either, even if the Space Corps couldn't fly in here during the storm.

Five years ago words like Australia, Turtle Scum, and Amebons held little meaning. I'd practiced insurance in the north of England. Eventually, I got drafted. Why bother with insurance, when an alien race tries to destroy a world because it's rich in uranium. I joined in. It wasn't only the Aussie's problem. Next they'd come for our British nuclear power plants and then where would we be?

I could have avoided the draft, but blasting away Amebons was liberating. Twice as tall as a man, these hairless tripods with their black, deep-set eyes were hard to kill. Their turtle beasts were even tougher. I loved hearing them all explode when we sent them to their next world. My life was nothing before then. The Land Corps had to be the best thing ever to happen to me since Tommy went missing.

Not long before that, now a lifetime ago now, everything in my life soured. Daniela and I were out walking with our son, Tommy. I can still remember the smell of the tropical heat, the feel of my shirt, hot and clammy on my back. We had argued, so I had hung back to calm down.

That's when they tried to kidnap Tommy.

It was clever the way a local man snuck up behind him. Tommy was ten years old back then, and I'm sure he was daydreaming, or watching the elephants trundle along the steamy, crowded road. All the locals touched him, it was a cultural thing, and he never noticed the small black-haired man.

He didn't resist when he was seduced away far enough to break his mother's grip.

Daniela never noticed the small local boy step forward and offer his hand. She took it instinctively.

I strode forward, held Tommy's shoulder, and my vice-like grip tightened on the man's arm.

The local glanced over at me, and I threw him my darkest stare. It was enough, and small brown eyes acknowledged defeat. He half-smiled, let go of Tommy and darted through a doorway.

That was the first time I'd ever seen an Amebon up close. Sweat covered its dark, jelly-like skin, and I stared into its single eye, convinced I could see disappointment. It typed commands into an armored data entry screen built into its arm, and I wondered what their interest was in our children.

I was thankful the elephants hadn't distracted me. Afterwards we argued because she hadn't noticed what happened. I don't know why I never let it go, and after the cracks had appeared in our relationship, she took Tommy, and I never saw him again. To this day I blame every Amebon.

A lot of children went missing that year and rumors surfaced about the Amebons harvesting humans for growth plates to create a blended race better suited to Earth. In my lonely, self-imposed isolation, I took comfort in Tommy's escape. Wherever he was now, at least he had choices.

When they invaded. I wanted to send them a message. I wanted everyone to have choices. If anyone planned to ruin the Earth, it would be us, not some jelly-like, three-legged alien from forty light-years away. I joined the Corps to release my pent up frustration. What better way than to blast the guts out of a race that thought less of you because they travelled through space and had enslaved six other planets along the way. If I had my way, I would have—

"Grenade!" yelled Burt.

I threw myself down instinctively, and I chewed on sand. I covered my ears, and the pain flared in my arm. I squeezed the Bitch tight, as if it would fight back and take its vengeance when it had the chance...

Bert stared out past the blue-grey saltbush to his grenade. He ducked down beside me and covered his ears. Moments later the sonic explosion shook the surrounding ground, and Amebons screamed. Eventually I could hear the eagle's calls above while they soured on the hot thermals.

A noise to my right forced me upright, and I gritted my teeth against the pain and cursed as two Amebons appeared. I aimed instinctively from the hip and let 'The Bitch' do her stuff. Metal fragments and ionic particles burst from the rifle's muzzle, and the Amebons dance like puppets on impact. Yellow blood splatters and screams followed. Better them than me, I thought, and couldn't stop the bitter smile that knotted the muscles in my face. I wiped my mouth with the back of my hand.

"This is the life, Don."

Bert's smile was contagious, but I could only nod. It was as if he casually sipped cocktails at the O's Mess. I don't know how he took the killing in his stride. Even with Tommy ever foremost in my mind, I still didn't have the stomach for it. I understood his military humor as only a soldier could.

He threw another canister and yelled, "Grenade!"

Once again, we ducked and waited for the frag to clear, and when I glanced over the sandy outcrop, my tenuous hold on the day vanished. A wall of giant six-legged turtles, each with an Amebon atop, darkened the afternoon sky.

"Call it in, Donny, we have to move," Bert demanded.

I grabbed the radio hand piece and slowed the speed of my voice. "Alpha Echo Five, this is Charlie Zulu Two. Scout team moving to rendezvous point zero dot four one three."

The radio squawked. "Roger that."

I shouldered the radio, fired off a salvo of rounds, and followed Bert at the double over the crest of the nearest hill like a soldier with everything and nothing to lose.

WE CLAMBERED TO THE rendezvous point, short of breath, when a section of Amebons stepped from cover. They forced us to turn and retreat in a deadly cycle of fight, hide, and evade. We took the high ground, and I trained 'the Bitch' on a narrow passage between a rocky outcrop and waited for them to appear. A shot rang out from behind me, and I felt the tug of an Amebon's poisoned slug smack my leg. I fell and cursed my luck, convinced a sniper had hit me. The Amebons were getting smarter. Perhaps they had finally downloaded new fighting styles from the northern battles, but whatever it was, I believed we'd lost our tactical edge.

I threw Bert an ugly smile, and he dragged me to cover. We both knew there was no antidote left, so he strapped a bandage tight around my thigh.

I sat and fought the rising pain while Bert raised his head as high as he dared. He scanned the rocky silt outcrops, and his face betrayed concern. "Damn it! There's a pod of Amebons at eleven o'clock, Donny. There's too many and they've got the high ground." He pulled out a worn packet of smokes, lit one, stuck it in his mouth and smiled. I knew it was grim. Burt hadn't smoked for years, and I remember him saying that at his final battle he would pull out that old packet and die with one in his mouth.

"Call in fire support," he said, no longer smiling, and he tossed the cigarette.

I nodded.

Bert crawled up the hill, and I worked the radio. I fiddled with the controls until it crackled into life, but it had seen better days. The battery was almost dead.

"Send in reinforcements," I demanded and sent our encoded GPS coordinates.

"Roger that." The reply was faint.

I squeezed the mike again. "Intel for J2. Amebons using snipers."

"Acknowledged. Wilco. Are you—"

"Movement, Donny! Keep your head down." Bert fired a salvo of rounds, and I ducked.

"Reinforcements on way," I said and pulled out the radio's solar charger.

He nodded and continued his methodical search of the high ground. Around us everything went quiet.

I lay down, perched on my elbows, with The Bitch pointed forward and waited in eerie silence.

The sun stung the back of my neck, and a line of ants marched past, unaware of our plight. I stared at the ordered procession in wonder and considered that perhaps we weren't as important as we thought.

I must have drifted off because a sound startled me. Bert raised his rifle. "Goddammit! We've got to go."

I shook my head. "I'm not going anywhere on this leg."

I knew he understood.

THE POISON DISTORTED my hold on time, and my head spun. My leg developed a pulse of its own. The Amebons played leapfrog and closed in on us. I stood and fired. I lost count of how many rounds I'd used, of how many times I'd saved Bert and of how many times he had saved me. Today chaos ruled. If only I was a butterfly who could flap its wings and change the world, but my proverbial 'wings' were clipped. My gun stopped as I exhausted my rounds. This was the end of the line for me, and I didn't care anymore.

I heard a noise behind me and cursed. They must have circled us. "Bert! " I cried. "Another mag!" I held out my hand, and he threw me a spare. I caught it. Pain flared in my arm. I rammed the mag home and turned 'The Bitch' around to fire.

Three goddamn giants in sandy camouflage suits appeared, not Amebons, a Special Forces detachment of the Space Corps.

Relief coursed through me, and I sat down on a rock protruding from the sand. "Move over granddad," said the young, cocky SF soldier.

I shuffled over, and he sat alongside me on the rock. "HQ said you needed help. We're here to bring you back."

I glanced at Bert and grinned. These guys were something else. Sleeves rolled up, their muscles rippled from arms the size of my calves, and they acted like they owned the world.

Perhaps they did.

"Enemy," said one of the Special Forces guys.

They stood, guns forward, and fired at the Amebons. Bert checked his ammo and handed me another full mag.

I sighed, and we stood and fired at the Amebons, and I have to say I appreciated the support. There we were, young and old men alike, Space and Land Corp. I had a feeling our odds had improved.

The SF guys were better equipped than us, with more network-centric tech than the Amebons. GPS trackers, Kevlar reinforced camm suits with in-built EM generation plates and beyond-visual-horizon viewers. They had all the stuff Land Forces couldn't afford. These guys were surgical, and their laser-sighted rounds hit their mark with every shot. Legs, guts and dome-shaped heads went yellow and burst open like fractured watermelons. I had to admit it. You had to like these guys. The noise was deafening, and the smell of gunfire caught the back of my throat. I did my best. My efforts were a token gesture. The rush of adrenalin was enough to push back the effects of the poison, and I knew I'd suffer later.

When the one closest to me took a hit and fell. I ducked down and crawled over to him.

He yelled over the rifle fire. "Sniper at 1 o'clock, Smithie. Take him out."

"Roger that." The response from the biggest soldier was calm, almost monotone. I pulled the antidote out from his medi-pack and stabbed him with the antigen. I pulled out a bandage to bind his arm, but he stopped me. "Later," he said.

I nodded. He was stronger than I imagined, and as he stood, blood oozed from his wound. He ran forward and spurred everyone on to fight even harder. I stood, bit down on the pain and followed. The poison in my system robbed my strength, and I did my best to keep up. My eyesight blurred. I fired until I couldn't see well enough, and I sat down and gave in to the pain.

Bert turned up, exhausted. He tossed his cigarette and ground it into the sandy soil. He sat beside me.

"How's it going?" I asked.

He chuckled. "It's done, I guess. They're just having fun now. You know, Space Corp pussies."

I noticed the bullet wound in his leg and pointed. "Taken any antigen, Bert?"

He shook his head. "I'll wait, I'm not about to follow them."

I nodded and held my stomach tight. I knew the poison in me had spread enough to do its job. We knew these Special Forces guys weren't pussies, and the battle wasn't over yet. Bert meant that *we* were done. At that moment I couldn't be more appreciative of these guys, they really made a difference.

I sat and watched the sand particles in the wind settle into the folds of my camms, and I wondered how long it would take to cover the dead.

"SNIPER'S DEAD! REMAINING Amebons bugged out," said the Space Corp soldier I had tried to bandage.

I nodded. From where he stood, his immense frame blocked the sun.

"You put up an impressive fight, old man," said the biggest Space Corp guy, the one I had labeled as the cocky young one. They just looked tired now.

He wore his corporal's stripes with pride, and I didn't know what it was, the inflection of his voice, or the way he stood, it plucked at a memory I couldn't pin down. "Who the hell are you guys?" I said.

The Corporal lowered his Mk IV Sonic Machine Gun, the latest version; it made mine look like a toy." I'm Corporal Smyth." He pointed. "These are my men, Red and Macka." He grinned at me.

I frowned, confused over the name.

"And who the hell are you, Captain?" he said in the same cocky tone. "What in god's name are you doing this far forward? Damn Land Corps. Are you trying to win the war on your own?" He fed another canister into his machine gun..

I shook my head and caught a sense of looking into a distorted mirror. "*Smyth-Wilson...*"

He laughed and thrust out his hand. "It's a long way from the tropics, Dad."

"Tommy?" I took his offered hand, leaned forward to get a better look and emotions within me bubbled over.

I threw him a lopsided grin; thrilled he'd become the man I had hoped he would.

"What a place for a reunion."

I nodded, and we embraced—like soldiers—more a quick bear hug. My sight had all but failed. I was almost certain there was a tear in his eye.

I breathed in courage and asked that haunted me for more than a decade. "How's your mum?"

He grinned, unbuttoned his top pocket, and he handed me a photograph.

I recognized the picture from another time, of Daniela, Tommy, and I standing in front of the elephants. I struggled to smile.

"Mum copied it for luck. She wouldn't part with the original."

Emotion clawed at my throat. "Why? She left me—"

He shrugged. "I looked for you..."

I nodded. It hurt. "I should never have stopped looking for you," I said.

"You know how stubborn she is. She still loves you."

Speechless, I handed back the worn photograph.

"We'll get you patched up and I'll take you home."

I shook my head. "I'm done, Tommy. Tell her, that in my way, I never stopped loving her."

BERT HAD FALLEN ASLEEP, and he never woke. I found out he'd taken a poisoned round about the time I'd been shot and injected me with the last of his antigen. He never said. He was like that, selfless to his last breath.

I took comfort in Tommy's presence and the image of my son remained long after the light faded. I remembered Bert had a daughter and from the pictures I'd seen, she looked mighty fine. "Tommy, do something for me?"

"Sure, Dad. Name it."

"Tell Bert's daughter, Amelia, that if it weren't for him, I'd never lived long enough to see you again."

"I'd be honored to tell her of the day I discovered loyal soldiers in the desert."

I swallowed hard, nodded, and I gave in to the pain. I knew he would continue the fight and protect the Earth from this invasion, and I wondered what would happen if my Tommy fell in love with Bert's beautiful Amelia, wouldn't they have a story for their children one day? The thought took me into the next world.

ABOUT THE PUBLICATIONS

Indulge me this short monologue about my writing.

I have to start by saying that I'm humbled that you should be here to read this collective work, and I thank you for your support if you've purchased it. I've done this publication because I didn't want the work to be lost. I've heard some people say that as we learn how to write that most storytellers edit their work to the point where they remove their voice. I can only hope that in these stories, which are a collection of my early struggle to come to terms with the complexities of the craft, that I did not remove my voice from the story.

Yes, these are early pieces, and I have more work to submit – larger pieces – but I started off writing very short 50+ word stories and I wanted to preserve those tales that were bigger 500+ words before I began to write very large works. These ones at least can be read in small chunks of time.

If you will indulge me, I'll take a moment to go back to the beginning for me: back to 2001, when I finished the then final fantasy story from Robert Jordan's series, The Wheel of Time, and being a big fan of Marion Zimmerman Bradley (who had also stopped writing) was stuck for reading material. So my wife, Olivia, said if I couldn't find anything to read that I should write my own story. I have a lot to thank her for that and on that New Years Day I began writing and have never stopped. I wrote two and a half books (230K words) of a fantasy story and had people review it before I realized that I needed to improve my craft. While I was doing a science degree, I stumbled on a subject with Curtin

University where I had I had to read and analyze the science in science fiction, I fell in love with science fiction. I put the novel aside and wrote my first science fiction story entitled Gaia's Virus, (which I will publish separately when I get the rights back later this year) and I have not stepped back from my love of writing science (fiction) since.

What follows are the early years, my struggle with the craft, but I hope that you can find something within these stories that entertains you, something that pushes the boundaries of human desire or science, and makes you think.

THANK YOU
David Kernot
Author
2013

DEAD MAN WALKING: *first published in Black House Comics, 2011.*

A few years ago I used to travel to Canada from Australia quite regularly, and a good friend Captain, now Major, Erik Couture convinced me to start listening to the "This Week In Technology" (TWIT) podcasts. I kind of got hooked on the bio-engineering series (Futures in Biotech) and the hunt for the structure of DNA: in particular the sequencing of the human gene structure with Dr. Svente Paabo, and his team from the Max Planck Institute for Evolutionary Anthropology. I think while walking to the train each morning and listening to TWIT, this story grew from there. The story did earn me an Honourable Mention from the Writers of the Future Competition (and I'm pretty proud of that), and it was also published by Black House Comics back in 2011.

Review from Scary Minds Feb12: "Bringing in the Sci-Fi elements Dead Man Walking by David Kernot goes in an entirely unexpected resurrection tangent, all about the science don't you know, and throws one hell of a decision at the feet of the protagonist, Jonah. Kernot has a very visual style, which is pretty much space opera influenced in my unworthy opinion, so I was rocking on beyond the stars with this one." http://www.scaryminds.com/reviews/2012/magazine19.php

THE SCARLET RUNNERS: accepted for publication in Abandoned Towers Magazine, but it never appeared on their web page.

PICTURES OF ANOTHER Time: first published in Aoife's Kiss, March 2012.

GENESIS: this was the winning story from the United Federation of Planets Fan Club of South Australia, and first published on their web site in November 2006.

There are some stories that stick out in your mind: I remember coming home from work late in the day some time after submitting this story, and my wife, Olivia, answered the phone with a confused look on her face... There's a woman on the phone for you, she said, about a competition. She shrugged. I grabbed the phone, bewildered, only to find that I had won the competition. I was told that I had a talent, that I shouldn't give up writing, and that after reviewing many hundred submissions, my story had been selected as the winning one. I was elated. I think I received a prize of $250 for my efforts, although it may have only been $150, but $250 sticks in my *mind as the amount (I later found out it was in a book voucher) and I was told not to give up writing. The voice on the phone was quite complementary, and I was requested to attend their yearly Gala night, and be presented with my prize, which I did with great reservation. I'm not in to such things, but I have to say that amongst the dressed up science fiction movie characters, I took the stage, and accepted my cheque with thanks. It was an awesome moment that I've never forgotten. So here is the story, an early one and my first publication because they put it on their web site for a number of years.*

THE SENTINEL: *first published by AlienSkin Magazine, December 2006. You know those dreams you have where you die and then wake up hardly being able to breath? Well this one was after one of those, and it scared the living daylights out of me.*

WEDDING DRESS: *first published in AntipodeanSF Issue 108 May 2007. I used to walk from home to the train every day and spend my time thinking up new stories, and for a time I wrote a lot of 50 word stories, but this one was written after seeing a tarnished wedding dress in the window of the local second-hand shop I'd walk past each day. This was my first ever story published at Antipodean Science Fiction, and I have to say that over the years I've had a lot of stories published there, and learned a lot about writing thanks to Ion 'Nuke' Newcombe.*

CHICKEN SOUP: *first published in AntipodeanSF Issue 109 June 2007. About this time I was still into inline speed skating on roller blades, having been a keen roller skater all my life, and one time my wife, Olivia, and I*

headed out to the local indoor park – a mix of bike/skate and skate-board scene – it was filled with graffiti at the height of the Iraq War. The graffiti message had been sprayed across the main slating wall and it was hard to ignore.

ENTROPY: first published in AntipodeanSF Issue 115 Dec 2007.

GENESIS 1-6-8: first published in AntipodeanSF Issue 124 September 2008, as Genesis, but I've gone back and included the original quote from the bible.

REALITY IS: first published in AlienSkin Magazine in February 2009. After writing so many 50-word stories I tried to write five 100 word interconnected stories and this was the result.

STARRY EYED TRIO: there had been a lot of talk about the discovery of exo-planets in the media and Internet over the recent years and the trend was that they were able to discover ones that were smaller and closer to the Goldilocks zone from mammoth distances from earth. Gliese 581 hit the headlines with a furore and there was this SETI event where you could text a message to the aliens on Gliese. The message was assembled and punched out via radio link to the constellation containing the newly discovered Gliese series of exo-planets. It caused me to write the following 50 word story, which was the driver for then writing a collection of three joined stories

under the banner of Starry eyed trio. But here is the mini 50-worder, and then the stories that fell out of that. You may not have a telescope (unlike me) and may not stare at the night sky, so some of this wonder may be lost on you, and for that I apologise.

"Hello From Earth", first published in AntipodeanSF Issue 146 October 2009.

"Herschel" first published in AntipodeanSF Issue 146 August 2010.

"Space Twins" first published in AntipodeanSF Issue 147 September 2010.

"The Seven Sisters" first published in AntipodeanSF Issue 148 October 2010.

BEACH HOLIDAY: *first published in AntipodeanSF Issue 167 May 2012.*

WE STAND TOGETHER: *I often wondered what my grandfather, Bert, would have done after his journey to Australia as a civilian many years ago. While he was up working in the hot Australian desert during the nuclear tests, I wondered if he would have donned a uniform again and revert to his instinctive military training without a thought. I think that this idea (and while travelling in Asia and having my eldest son, Andrew, almost get kidnapped) was the genesis for this story. I hope you enjoy this future world story too.*

Don't miss out!

Visit the website below and you can sign up to receive emails whenever David Kernot publishes a new book. There's no charge and no obligation.

https://books2read.com/r/B-A-LKNUD-IVLHG

BOOKS 2 READ

Connecting independent readers to independent writers.

Did you love *The Early Years*? Then you should read *Panspermian Earth*[1] by David Kernot!

2

A novelette sized collection of eleven connected science fiction short stories around the theme of panspermia: the concept that life originated from space and is delivered through meteorites and comets falling onto a planet. Could humankind be contributing to this through our own interstellar explorations?

Read more at www.davidkernot.com.

---

1. https://books2read.com/u/bWaX71

2. https://books2read.com/u/bWaX71

Also by David Kernot

Beam Rider
The Early Years
Autumn Comes Slowly
Panspermian Earth
The Search for Giselle
Future Worlds
Gateway Through Time
Not Like Us

Watch for more at www.davidkernot.com.

About the Author

David Kernot is an Australian author living in the Mid North of South Australia. He writes contemporary fantasy, science and climate fiction, and horror, and is the author of over eighty published short stories in a variety of anthologies in Australia, the US, Canada, and the UK including the Year's Best Australian Fantasy & Horror, and Award Winning Australian Writing. He released his first dark sci-fi indie novel, Gateway Through Time in 2020. It joins a 2024 novella, Nor Like Us, two novelettes and five collections of short fiction. More information can be found at http://www.davidkernot.com

Read more at www.davidkernot.com.